OAK LAWN PUBLIC LIBRARY

3 1186 00830 5443

P9-DCR-584

For a very special bunny:

_____

Happy Birthday, Bunny!

Liz Garton Scanlon

illustrated by
Stephanie Graegin

MAR 1 1 2013

OAK LAWN LIBRARY

Beach Lane Books · New York London Toronto Sydney New Delhi

For Finlay and Willa, my birthday bunnies
—L. G. S.

For Bustopher and Pea
—S. G.

BEACH LANE BOOKS
An imprint of Simon & Schuster Children's Publishing Division
1230 Avenue of the Americas, New York, New York 10020
Text copyright © 2013 by Elizabeth Garton Scanlon
Illustrations copyright © 2013 by Stephanie Graegin
All rights reserved, including the right of reproduction in whole or in part in any form.
BEACH LANE BOOKS is a trademark of Simon & Schuster, Inc.
For information about special discounts for bulk purchases, please contact
Simon & Schuster Special Sales at 1-866-506-1949 or business@simonandschuster.com.
The Simon & Schuster Speakers Bureau can bring authors to your live event.
For more information or to book an event, contact the Simon & Schuster Speakers Bureau
at 1-866-248-3049 or visit our website at www.simonspeakers.com.
Book design by Lauren Rille
The text for this book is set in Canterbury Old Style.
The illustrations for this book are rendered in pencil and ink washes
and then assembled and colored digitally.
Manufactured in China
1012 SCP
First Edition
10 9 8 7 6 5 4 3 2 1
Library of Congress Cataloging-in-Publication Data
Scanlon, Elizabeth Garton.
Happy birthday, bunny! / Liz Garton Scanlon ; illustrated by Stephanie Graegin.—1st ed.
p. cm.
Summary: Illustrations and rhyming text portray the birthday party of a beloved baby.
ISBN 978-1-4424-0287-4 (hardcover)
ISBN 978-1-4424-4553-6 (eBook)
[1. Stories in rhyme. 2. Birthdays—Fiction. 3. Parties—Fiction. 4. Babies—Fiction.]
I. Graegin, Stephanie, ill. II. Title.
PZ8.3.S2798Hap 2013
[E]—dc23
2011018590

What are these
and what are those?

Fancy shoes and party clothes!

Someone's knocking—who is here?

Peekaboo, it's Nana, dear.

Why is everyone so loud?

Because we're all so thrilled and proud!

What's that pretty yellow glow?

Make a wish . . .

get set . . .

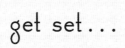

and blow!

What's this box and what's inside?

A rocking zebra—take a ride!

Why does everyone say *cheese?*

Because we want a picture, please!

What do you mean that time just flies?

You're growing up
before our eyes.

And is that it? My birthday's done?

Till *next* year, my sweet honey bun.